TEEN TITANS GO!®

Raintree

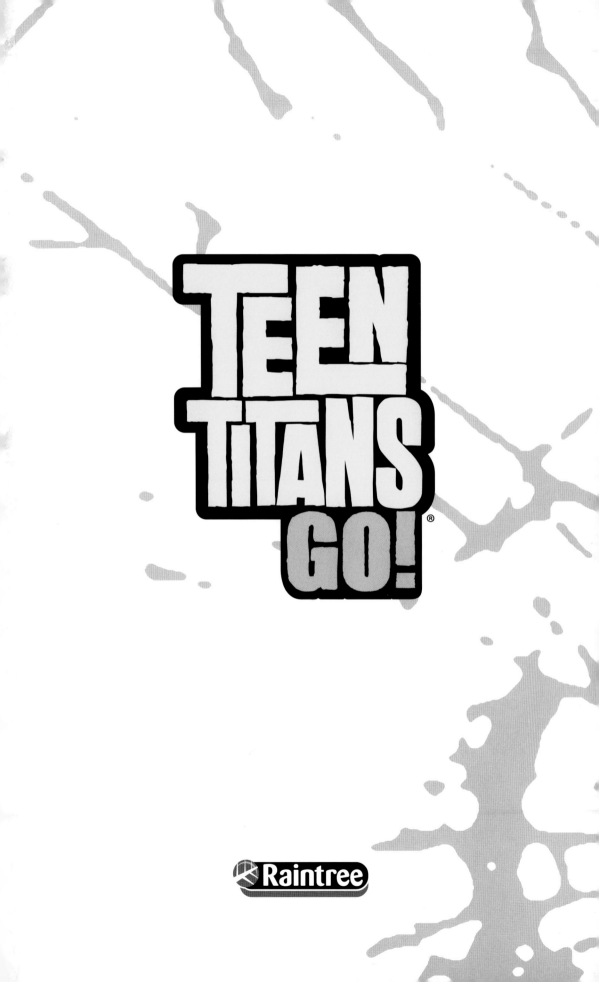

Raintree is an imprint of Capstone Global Library Limited, a company incorporated in England and Wales having its registered office at 7 Pilgrim Street, London, EC4V 6LB - Registered company number: 6695582

www.raintreepublishers.co.uk
myorders@raintreepublishers.co.uk

First published by Raintree in 2014

Ashley C. Andersen Zantop *Publisher*
Michael Dahl *Editorial Director*
Sean Tulien *Editor*
Heather Kindseth *Creative Director*
Alison Thiele *Designer*
Kathy McColley *Production Specialist*

DC COMICS
Kristy Quinn *Original U.S. Editor*

ISBN 978 1 406 27946 7

Printed in China by Nordica.
1013/CA21301918
17 16 15 14 13
10 9 8 7 6 5 4 3 2 1

A full catalogue record for this book is available from the British Library.

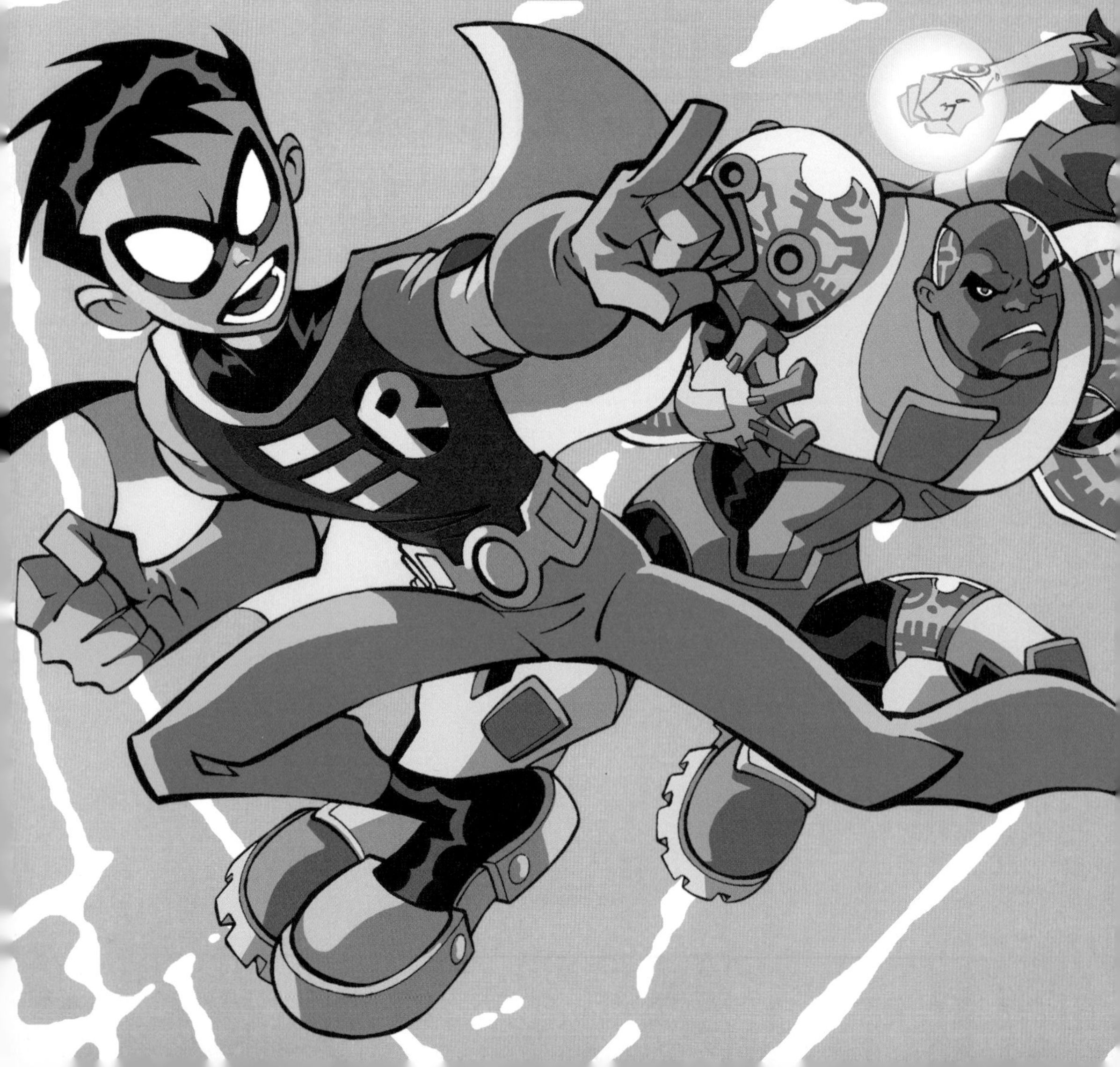

TEEN TITANS GO!®

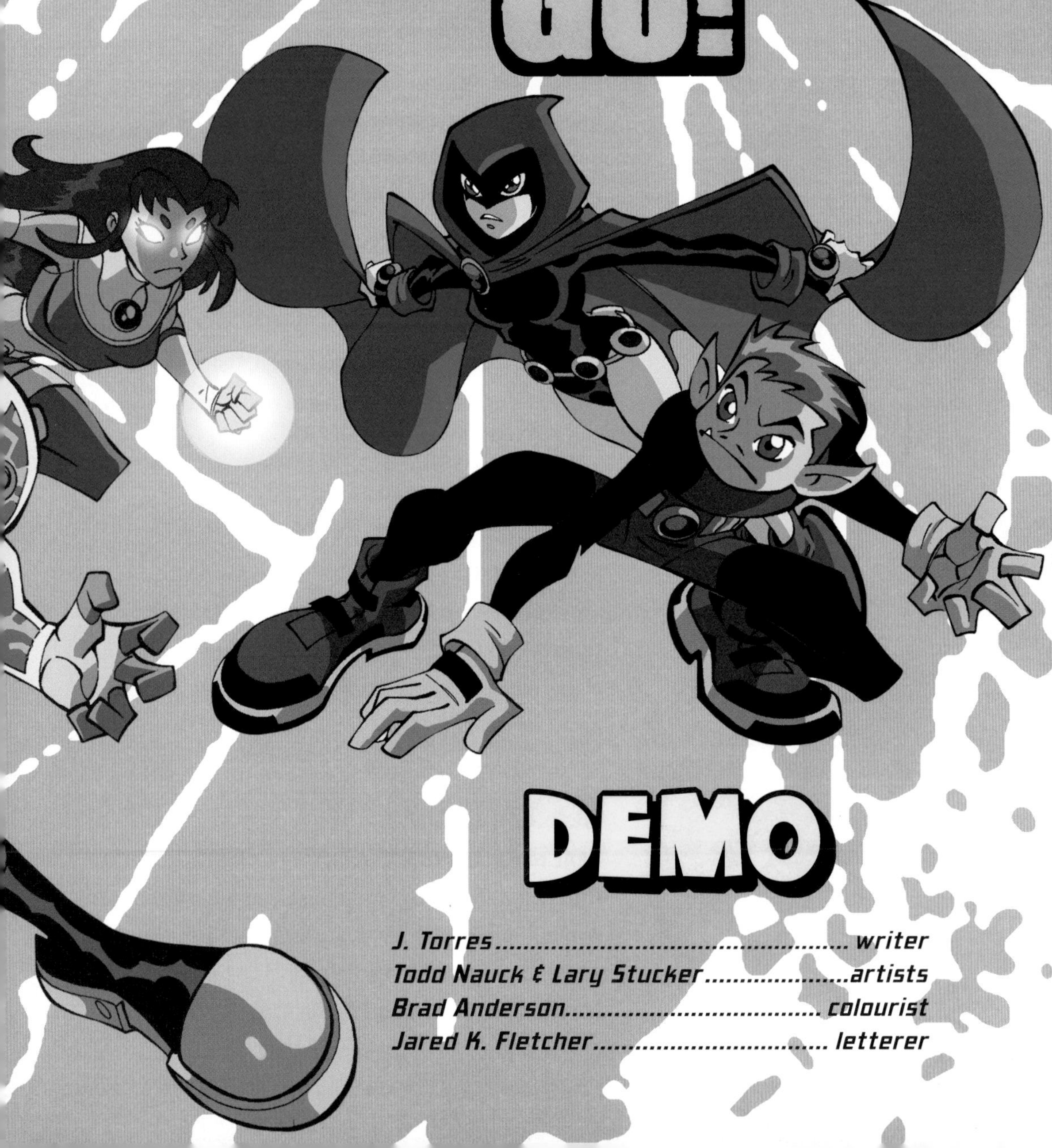

DEMO

J. Torres .... writer
Todd Nauck & Lary Stucker .... artists
Brad Anderson .... colourist
Jared K. Fletcher .... letterer

TEEN TITANS GO!

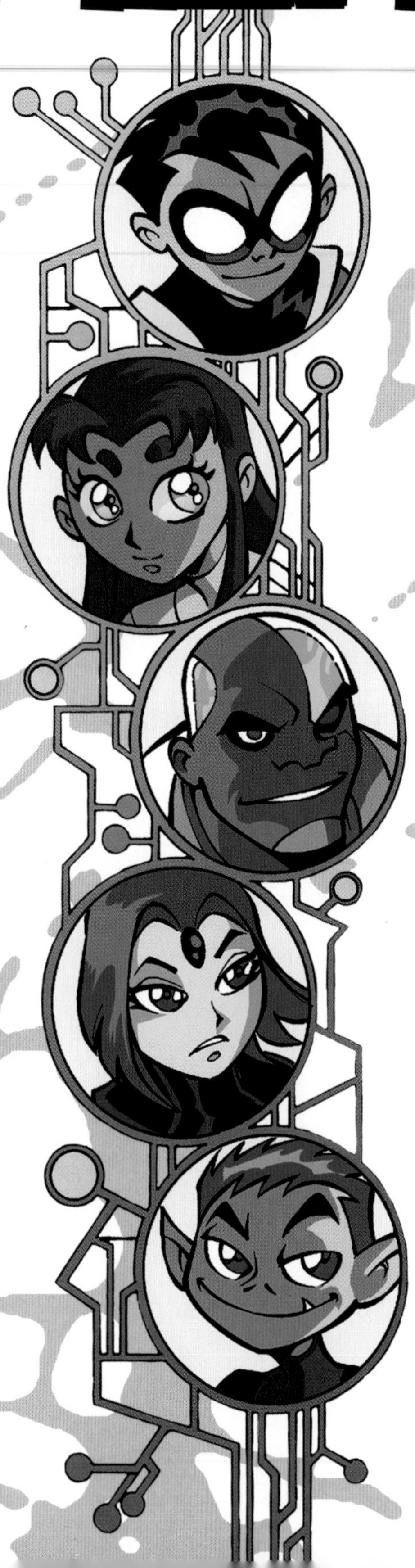

ROBIN

REAL NAME: Dick Grayson

BIO: The perfectionist leader of the group has one main complaint about his teammates: the other Titans just won't do what he says. As the partner of Batman, Robin is a talented acrobat, martial artist, and hacker.

STARFIRE

REAL NAME: Princess Koriand'r

BIO: Formerly a warrior Princess of the now-destroyed planet Tamaran, Starfire found a new home on Earth, and a new family in the Teen Titans.

CYBORG

REAL NAME: Victor Stone

BIO: Cyborg is a laid-back half teen, half robot who's more interested in eating pizza and playing video games than fighting crime.

RAVEN

REAL NAME: Raven

BIO: Raven is an Azarathian empath who can teleport and control her "soul-self," which can fight physically as well as act as Raven's eyes and ears away from her body.

BEAST BOY

REAL NAME: Garfield Logan

BIO: Beast Boy is Cyborg's best bud. He's a slightly dim but lovable loafer who can transform into all sorts of animals [when he's not too busy eating burritos and watching TV]. He's also a vegetarian.

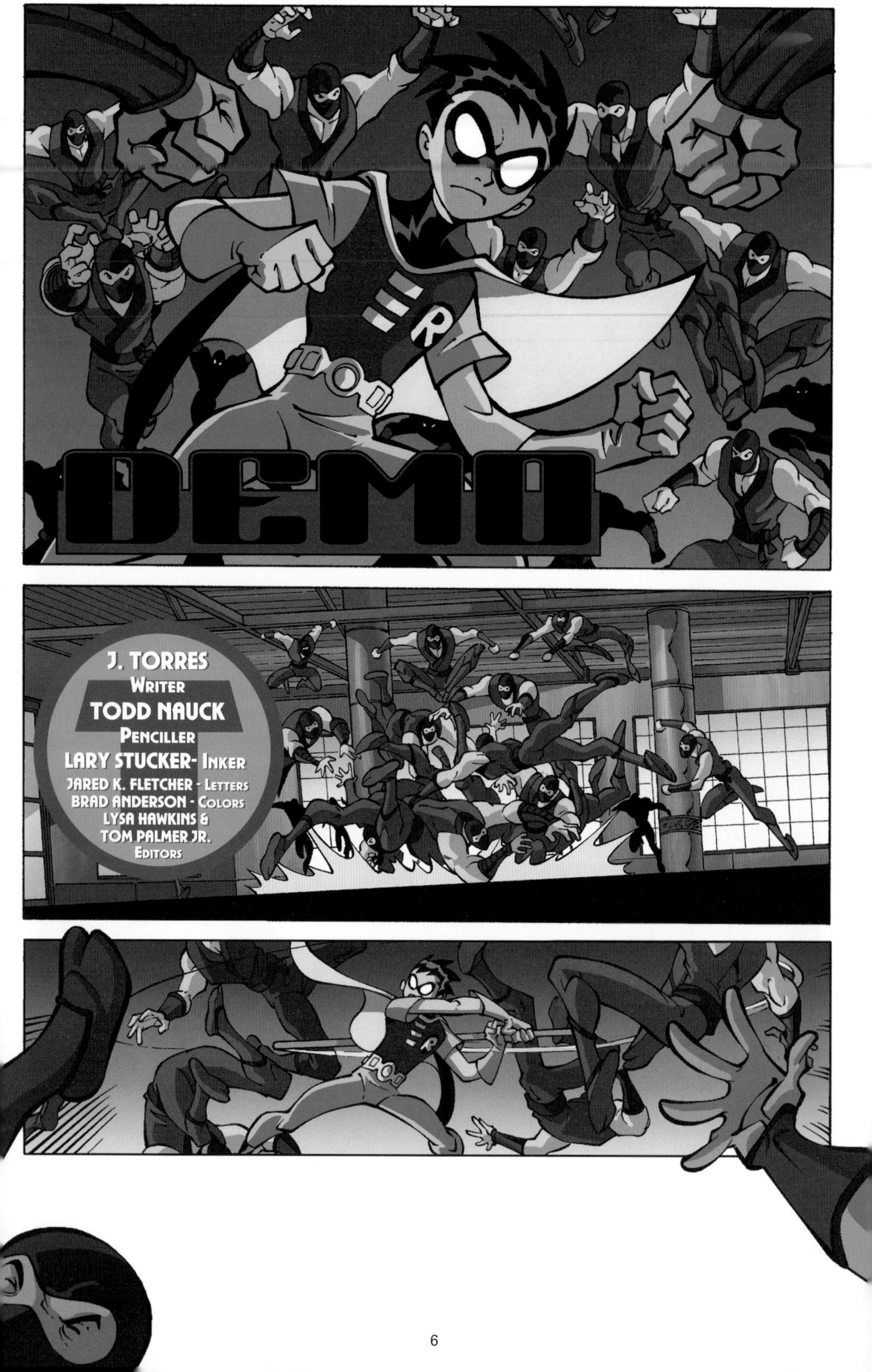
DEMO
J. TORRES
WRITER
TODD NAUCK
PENCILLER
LARY STUCKER- INKER
JARED K. FLETCHER - LETTERS
BRAD ANDERSON - COLORS
LYSA HAWKINS &
TOM PALMER JR.
EDITORS

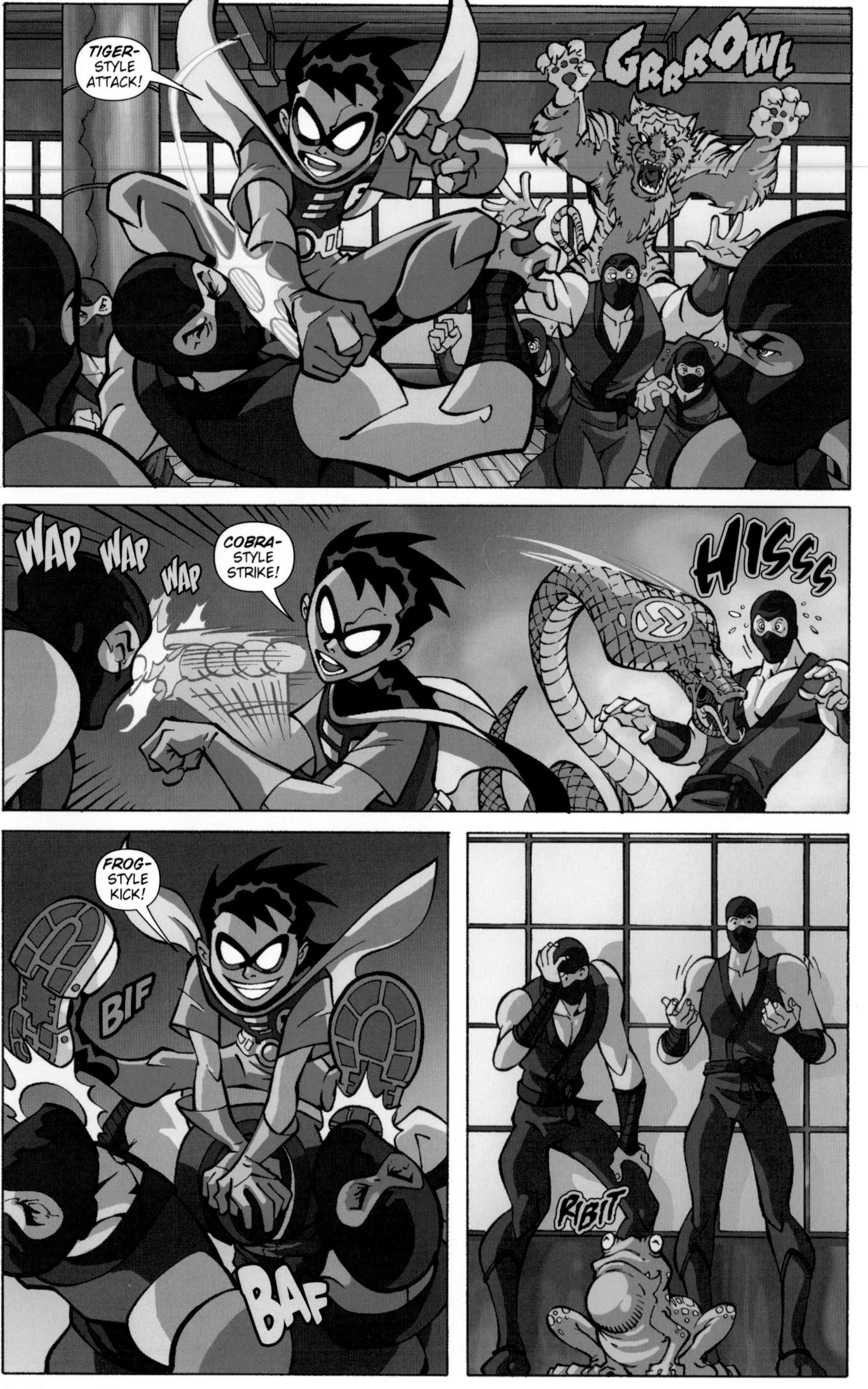
TIGER-STYLE ATTACK!
GRRROWL
WAP WAP WAP
COBRA-STYLE STRIKE!
HISSS
FROG-STYLE KICK!
BIF
BAF
RIBIT

H.A.E.Y.P.

WHY ARE WE WATCHING THE TEEN TITANS PLAY A *VIDEO GAME*?

IT'S ALL PART OF MY PLAN, *APE FACE*!

"SUPER NINJA FURY" IS NOT JUST SOME COOL MULTI-PLAYER ONLINE FIGHTING GAME...

...IT'S AN *INGENIOUS* PROGRAM THAT I WROTE TO RECORD AND ANALYZE THE TEEN TITANS' *FIGHTING MOVES*!

THE MORE THOSE PIT-SNIFFERS PLAY THE GAME, THE MORE "CHEAT CODES" I GET TO USE *AGAINST* THEM!

MY PROGRAM WILL TELL ME HOW THE SCRUM-BUFFERS BATTLE, HOW THEY THINK, IF THEY'LL PUNCH OR THEY'LL KICK, IF THEY'LL ZIG OR THEY'LL ZAG!

TAP TAP TAP TAP

MWA-HA-HA-HA!

13

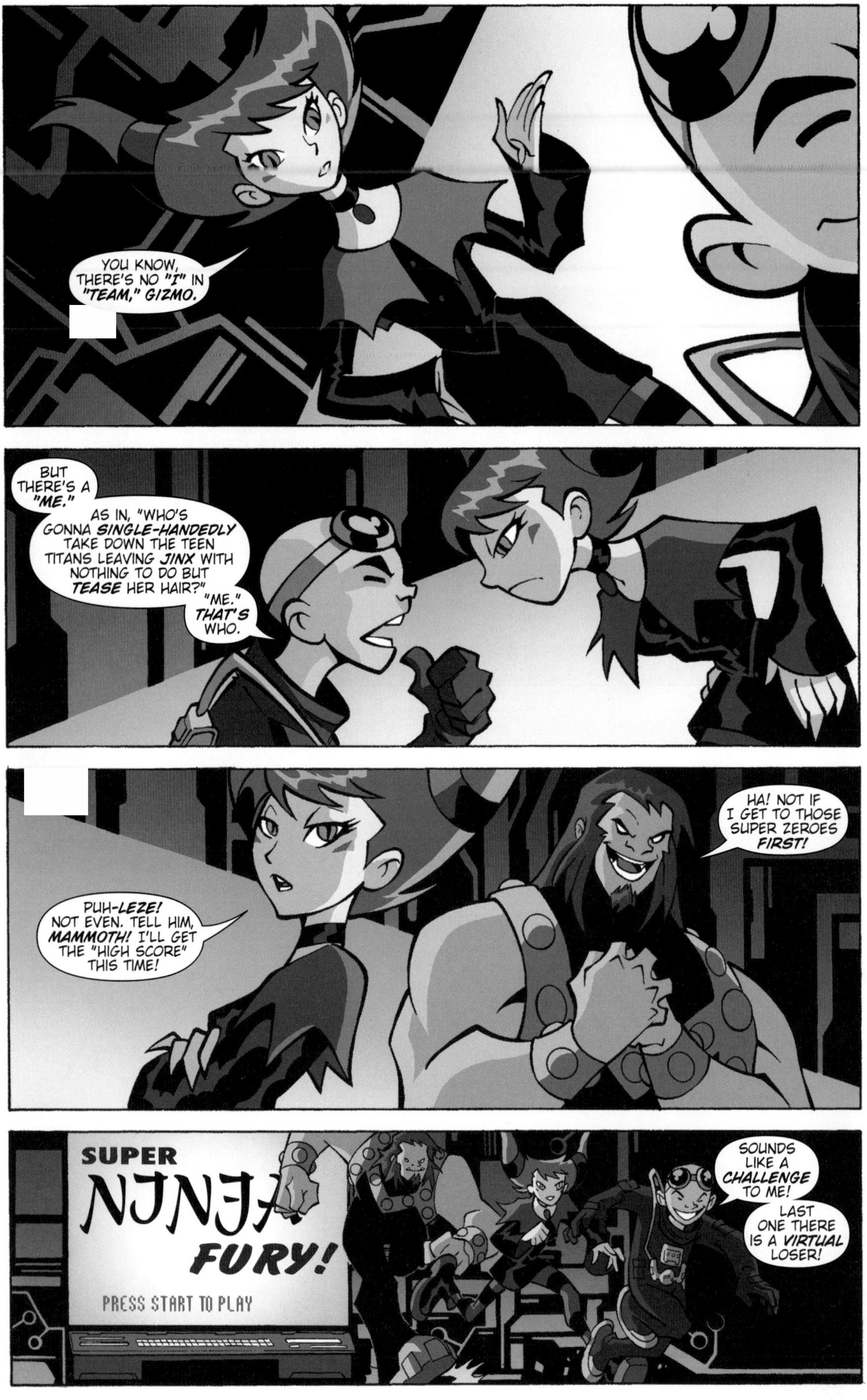
YOU KNOW, THERE'S NO "I" IN "TEAM," GIZMO.
BUT THERE'S A "ME."
AS IN, "WHO'S GONNA SINGLE-HANDEDLY TAKE DOWN THE TEEN TITANS LEAVING JINX WITH NOTHING TO DO BUT TEASE HER HAIR?"
"ME." THAT'S WHO.
HA! NOT IF I GET TO THOSE SUPER ZEROES FIRST!
PUH-LEZE! NOT EVEN. TELL HIM, MAMMOTH! I'LL GET THE "HIGH SCORE" THIS TIME!
SUPER
NINJA
FURY!
PRESS START TO PLAY
SOUNDS LIKE A CHALLENGE TO ME!
LAST ONE THERE IS A VIRTUAL LOSER!

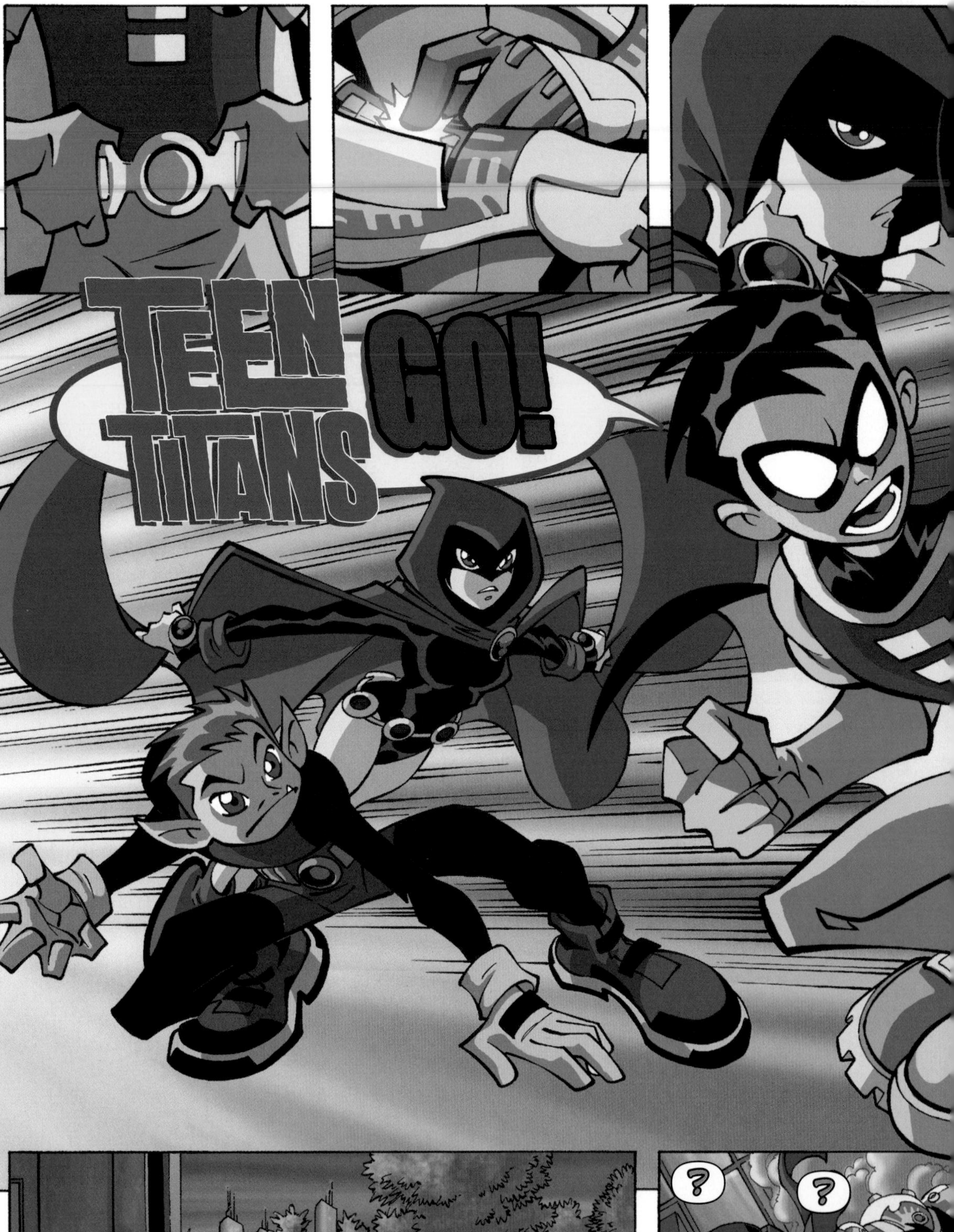
TEEN TITANS GO!
?
?
?

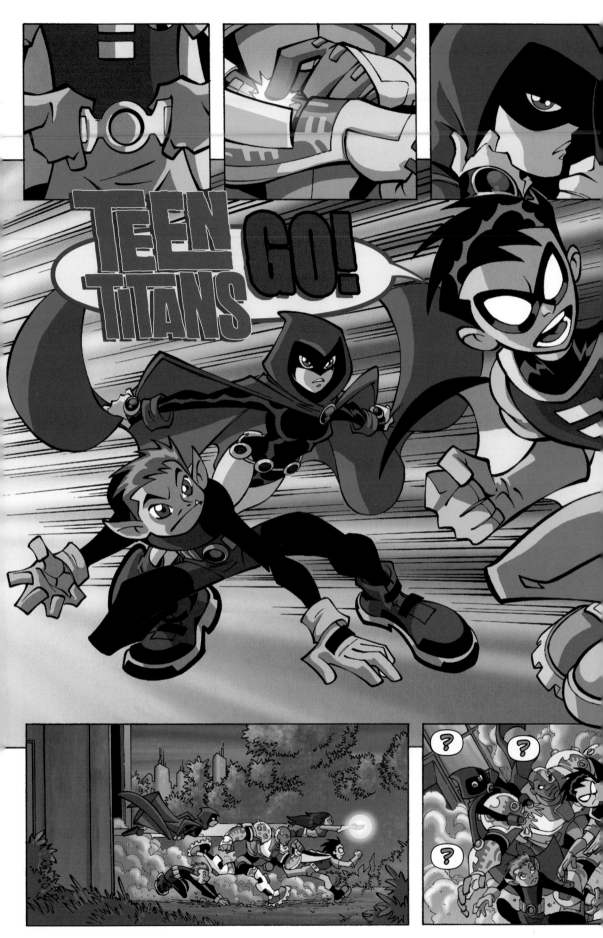

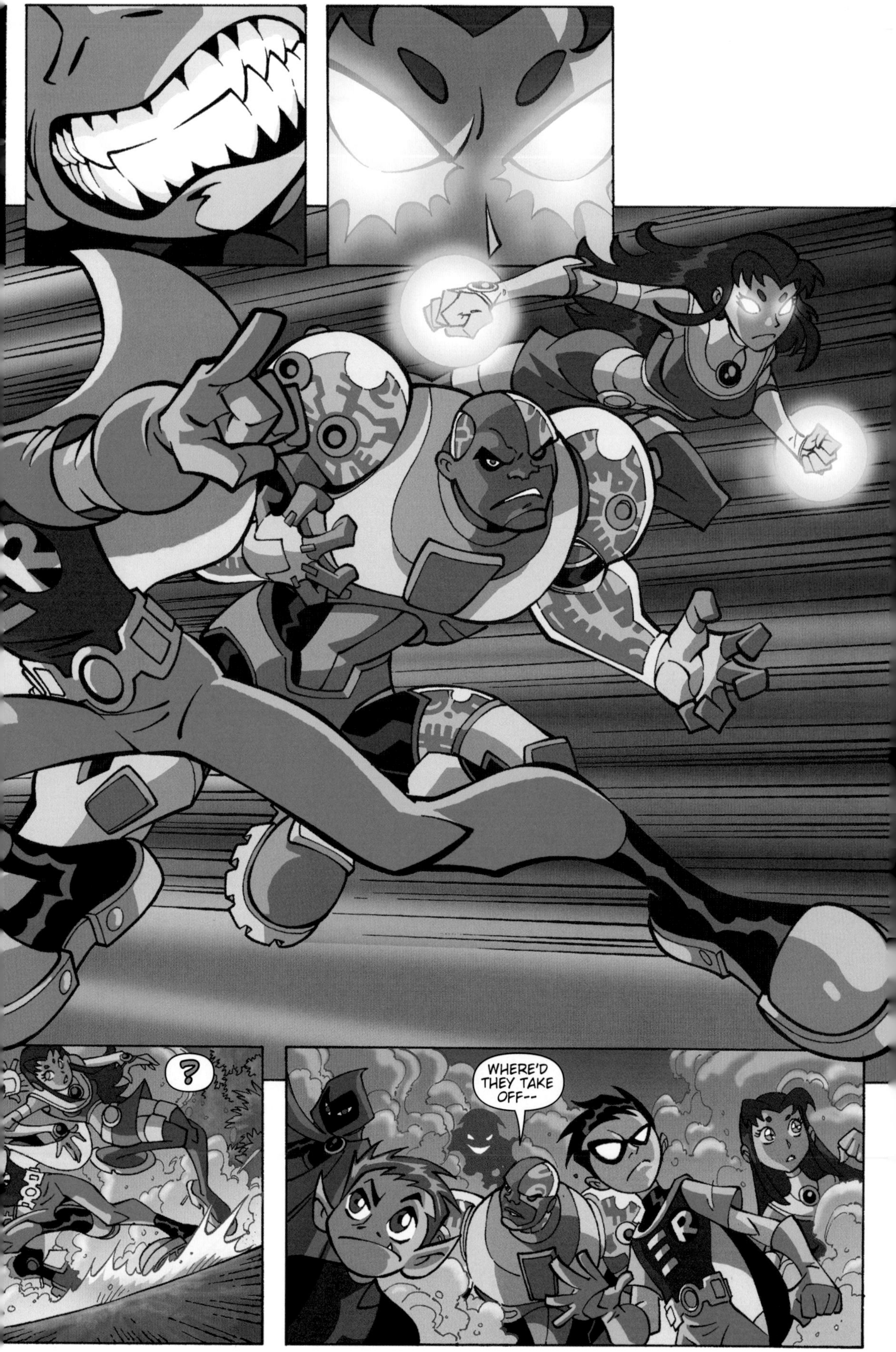
?
WHERE'D THEY TAKE OFF--

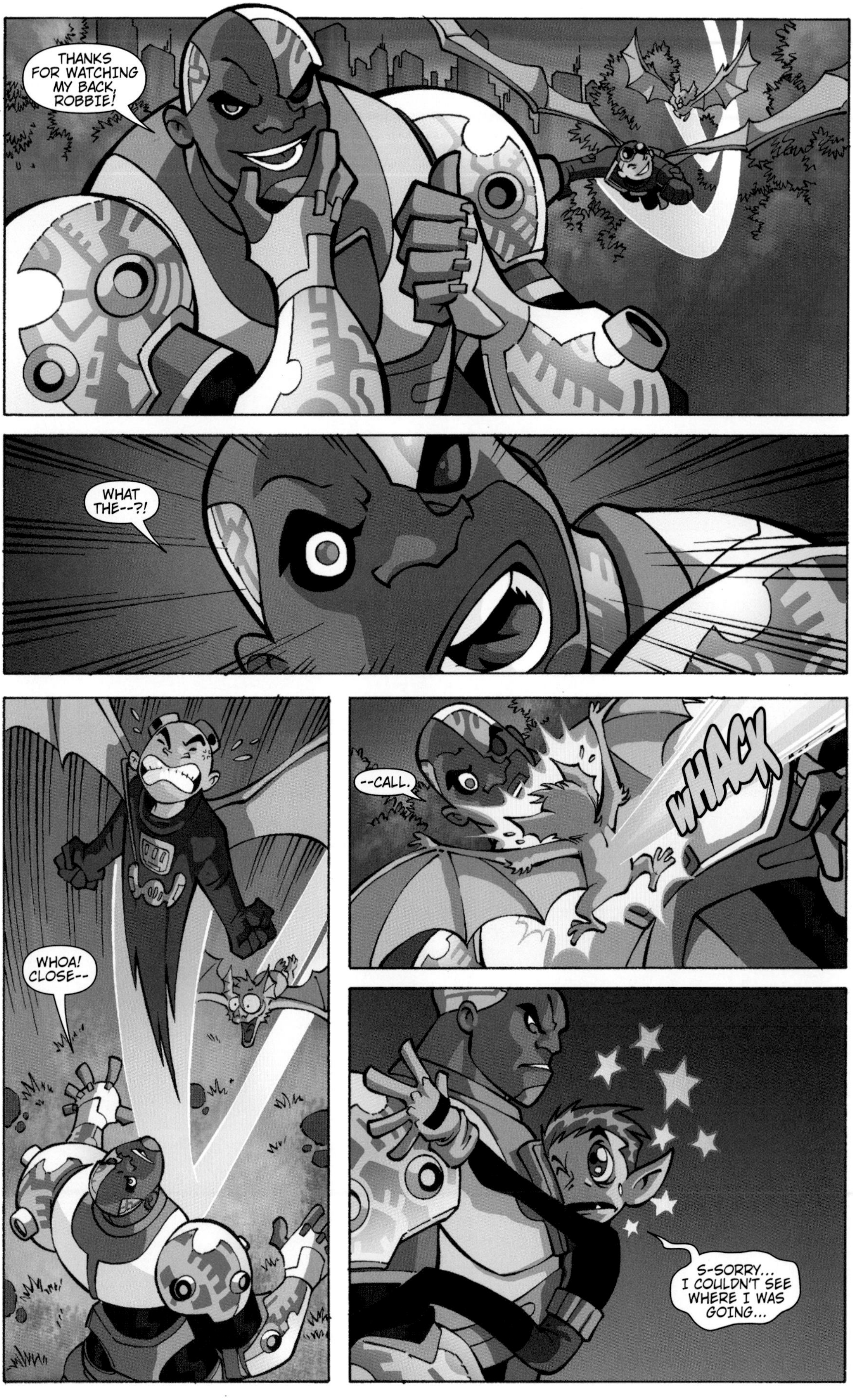
THANKS FOR WATCHING MY BACK, ROBBIE!
WHAT THE--?!
WHOA! CLOSE--
--CALL.
wHACK
S-SORRY... I COULDN'T SEE WHERE I WAS GOING...

BATTLE SIMULATION OVER
MISSION...
FAILED

AHEM.

MY APOLOGIES, MR. SLADE. THIS DEMONSTRATION OF OUR NEW PLAN TO TAKE DOWN THE TEEN TITANS DIDN'T EXACTLY GO AS, ER, PLANNED.

MAMMOTH	GIZMO	JINX
-26/594	-30/452	-18/70

PERHAPS THERE WAS A SLIGHT GLITCH IN THE PROGRAMMING AND THE TITANS' SIMULATED POWER LEVELS WERE SET A LITTLE TOO HIGH SO--

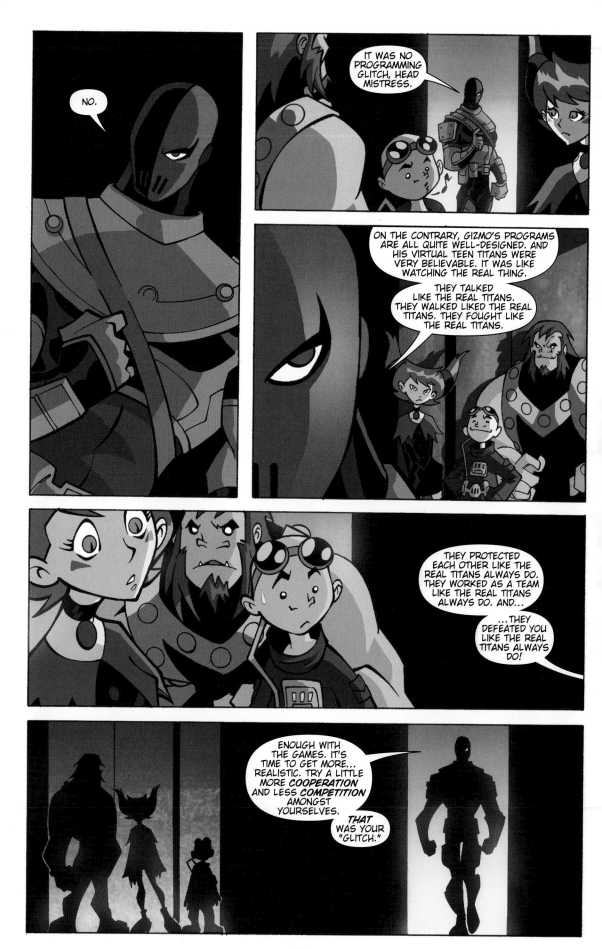

CREATORS

J. TORRES WRITER

J. Torres won the Shuster Award for Outstanding Writer for his work on Batman: Legends of the Dark Knight, Love As a Foreign Language, and Teen Titans Go! He is also the writer of the Eisner Award nominated Alison Dare and the YALSA listed Days Like This and Lola: A Ghost Story. Other comic book credits include Avatar: The Last Airbender, Batman: The Brave and the Bold, Legion of Super-Heroes in the 31st Century, Ninja Scroll, Wonder Girl, Wonder Woman, and WALL-E: Recharge.

TODD NAUCK ARTIST

Todd Nauck is an American comic book artist and writer. Nauck is most notable for his work on Young Justice, Teen Titans Go!, and his own creation, Wildguard.

GLOSSARY

cowardly – lacking courage

distress – a feeling of great discomfort, or in need of help

fury – violent anger or rage

glitch – any sudden thing that goes wrong or causes a problem, usually with machinery, as in a computer glitch

havoc – great damage and chaos

ingenious – clever or inventive

lame – weak or unconvincing

onslaught – overwhelming assault or attack

reflex – automatic action that happens without a person's control or effort

regroup – reform and reorganize for a second attack

simulate – create a realistic model of something

wreak -- carry out or inflict

VISUAL QUESTIONS & PROMPTS

I. On page 12, we see little ninjas running across the panel border, up the gutter, and into another panel on page 13. Why do you think this comic's creators did this? Explain your answer.

2. In the first panel, we see Beast Boy with birds flying around his head. In the second panel, we see drops of water dripping from his head. Based on these two facts, explain what you think Beast Boy is feeling in each panel. Reread page 10 if you need a hint.

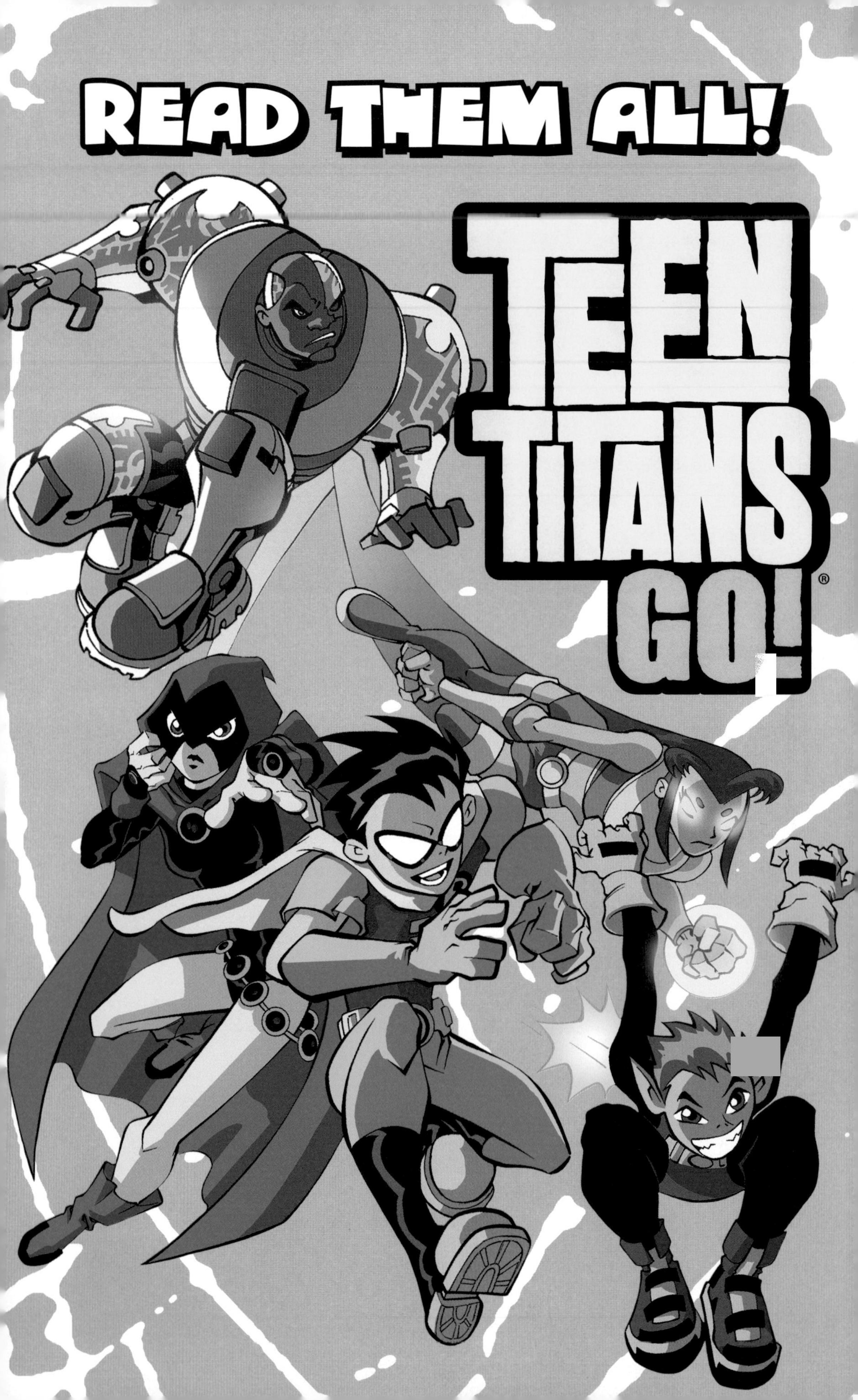
READ THEM ALL!
TEEN TITANS GO!

TEEN TITANS GO!®

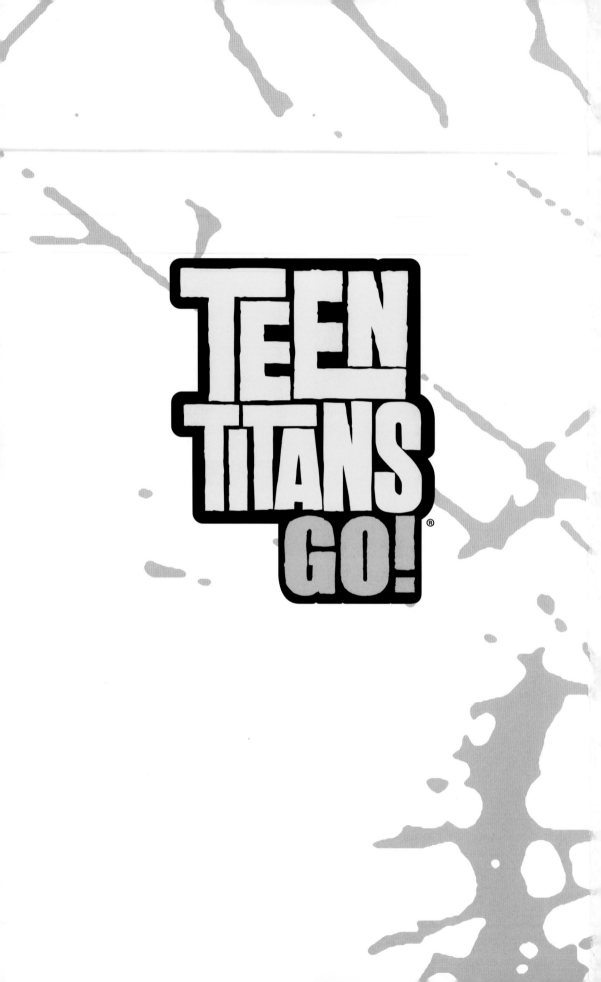